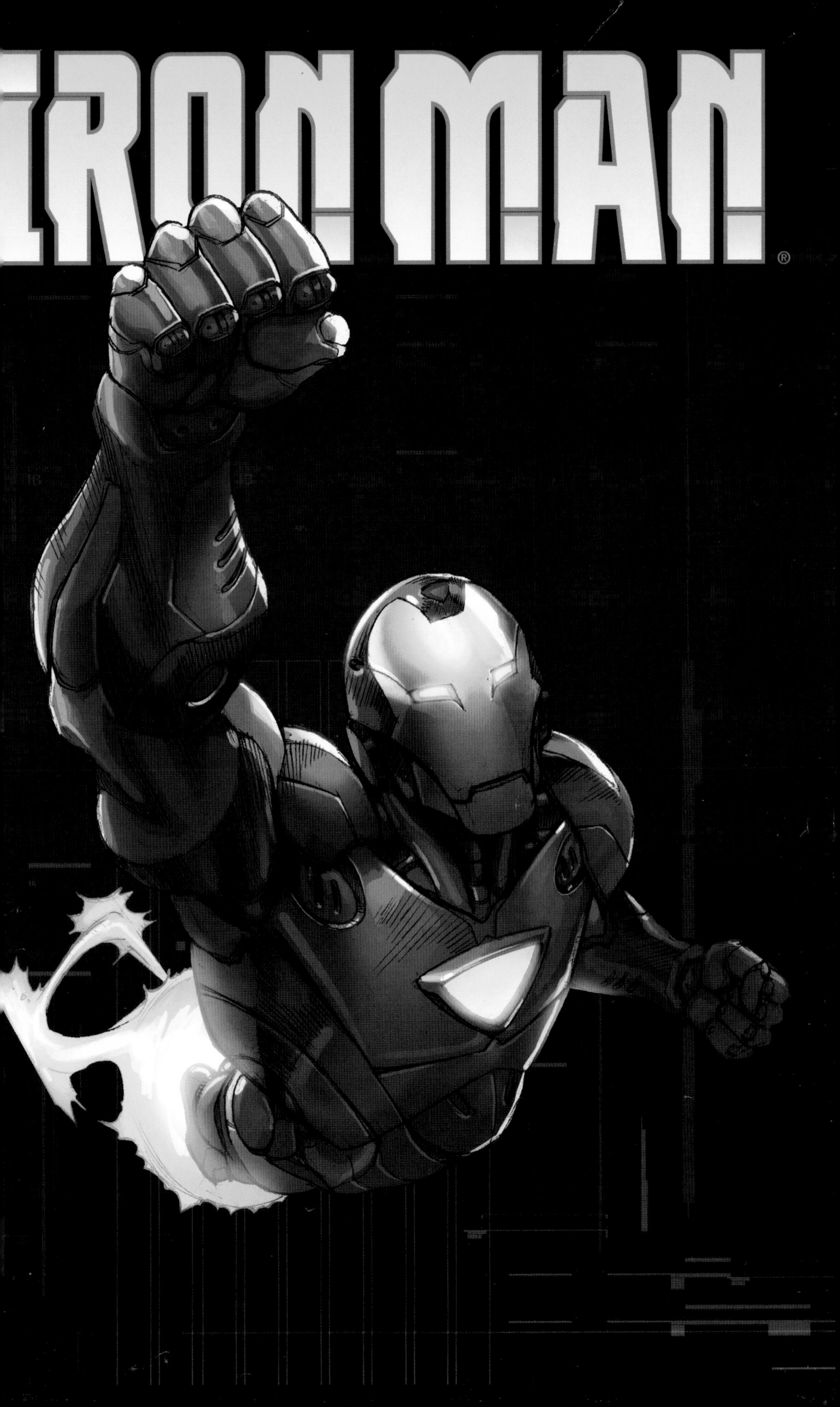
IRON MAN®

VISIT US AT
www.abdopublishing.com

Reinforced library bound edition published in 2011 by Spotlight, a division of the ABDO Group, 8000 West 78th Street, Edina, Minnesota 55439. Spotlight produces high-quality reinforced library bound editions for schools and libraries. Published by agreement with Marvel Characters, Inc.

Printed in the United States of America, Melrose Park, Illinois.
042010
092010
This book contains at least 10% recycled material.

Library of Congress Cataloging-in-Publication Data

Van Lente, Fred.
  Northern lights / story, Fred Van Lente ; art, Scott Koblish.
     p. cm. -- (Iron Man)
  "Marvel."
  ISBN 978-1-59961-773-2
  1. Graphic novels. [1. Graphic novels. 2. Superheroes--Fiction.] I. Koblish, Scott, ill. II. Title.
PZ7.7.V26Nor 2010
741.5'973--dc22
                              2009052838

All Spotlight books have reinforced library bindings and
are manufactured in the United States of America.

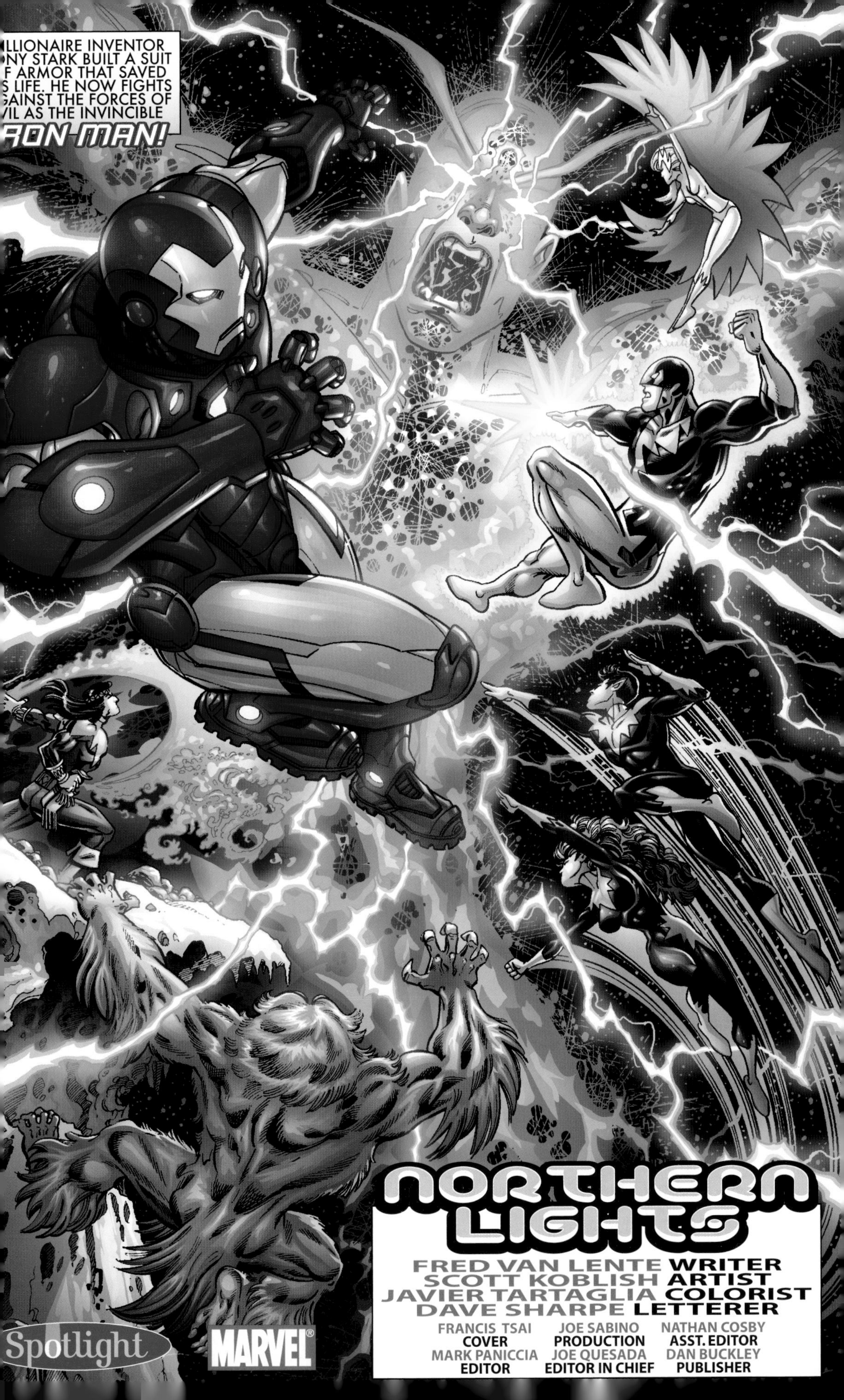
ILLIONAIRE INVENTOR
ONY STARK BUILT A SUIT
F ARMOR THAT SAVED
S LIFE. HE NOW FIGHTS
GAINST THE FORCES OF
VIL AS THE INVINCIBLE
RON MAN!
NORTHERN LIGHTS
FRED VAN LENTE WRITER
SCOTT KOBLISH ARTIST
JAVIER TARTAGLIA COLORIST
DAVE SHARPE LETTERER
FRANCIS TSAI COVER
JOE SABINO PRODUCTION
NATHAN COSBY ASST. EDITOR
MARK PANICCIA EDITOR
JOE QUESADA EDITOR IN CHIEF
DAN BUCKLEY PUBLISHER
Spotlight
MARVEL

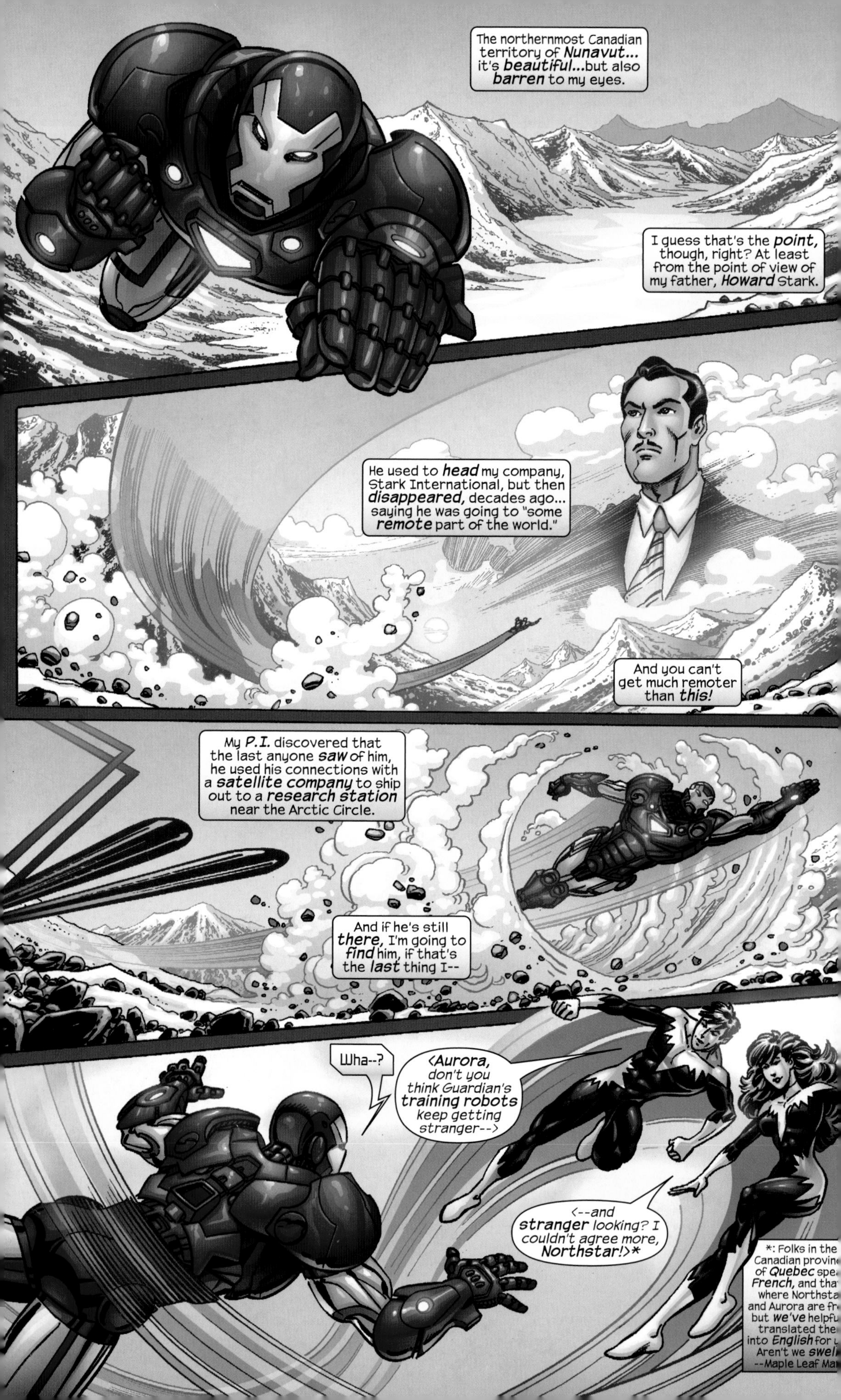

The northernmost Canadian territory of Nunavut... it's beautiful...but also barren to my eyes.
I guess that's the point, though, right? At least from the point of view of my father, Howard Stark.
He used to head my company, Stark International, but then disappeared, decades ago... saying he was going to "some remote part of the world."
And you can't get much remoter than this!
My P.I. discovered that the last anyone saw of him, he used his connections with a satellite company to ship out to a research station near the Arctic Circle.
And if he's still there, I'm going to find him, if that's the last thing I--
Wha--?
<Aurora, don't you think Guardian's training robots keep getting stranger-->
<--and stranger looking? I couldn't agree more, Northstar!>*
*: Folks in the Canadian provin of Quebec spe French, and tha where Northsta and Aurora are fr but we've helpfu translated the into English for u Aren't we swell --Maple Leaf Ma

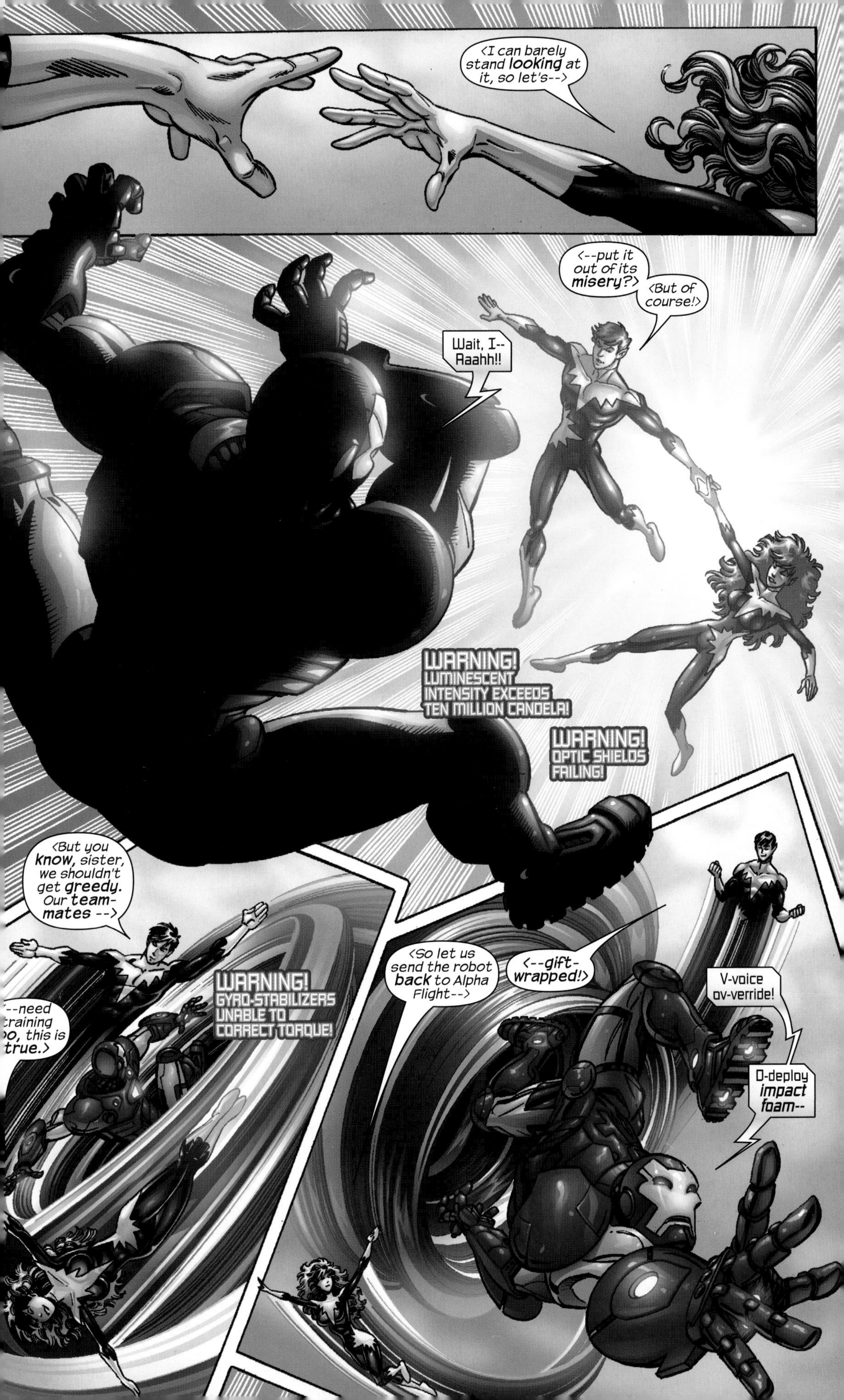

<I can barely stand looking at it, so let's-->
<--put it out of its misery?>
<But of course!>
Wait, I-- Raahh!!
WARNING! LUMINESCENT INTENSITY EXCEEDS TEN MILLION CANDELA!
WARNING! OPTIC SHIELDS FAILING!
<But you know, sister, we shouldn't get greedy. Our team-mates -->
--need training o, this is true.>
WARNING! GYRO-STABILIZERS UNABLE TO CORRECT TORQUE!
<So let us send the robot back to Alpha Flight-->
<--gift-wrapped!>
V-voice ov-verride!
D-deploy impact foam--

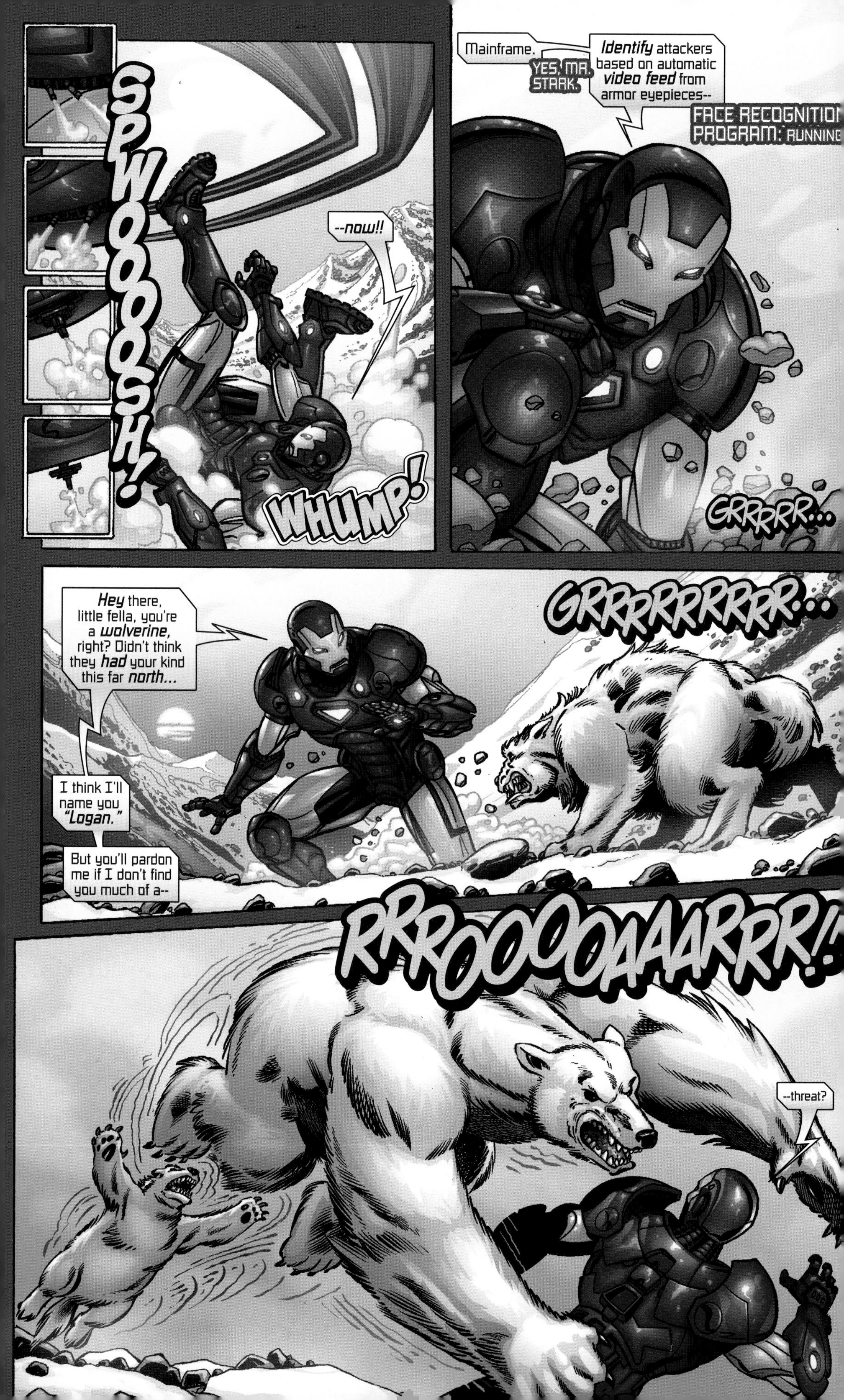
SPWOOOOSH!
--now!!
WHUMP!
Mainframe.
YES, MR. STARK.
Identify attackers based on automatic video feed from armor eyepieces--
FACE RECOGNITION PROGRAM: RUNNING
GRRRRR...
Hey there, little fella, you're a wolverine, right? Didn't think they had your kind this far north...
I think I'll name you "Logan."
But you'll pardon me if I don't find you much of a--
GRRRRRRRRR...
RRROOOOAAARRR!
--threat?

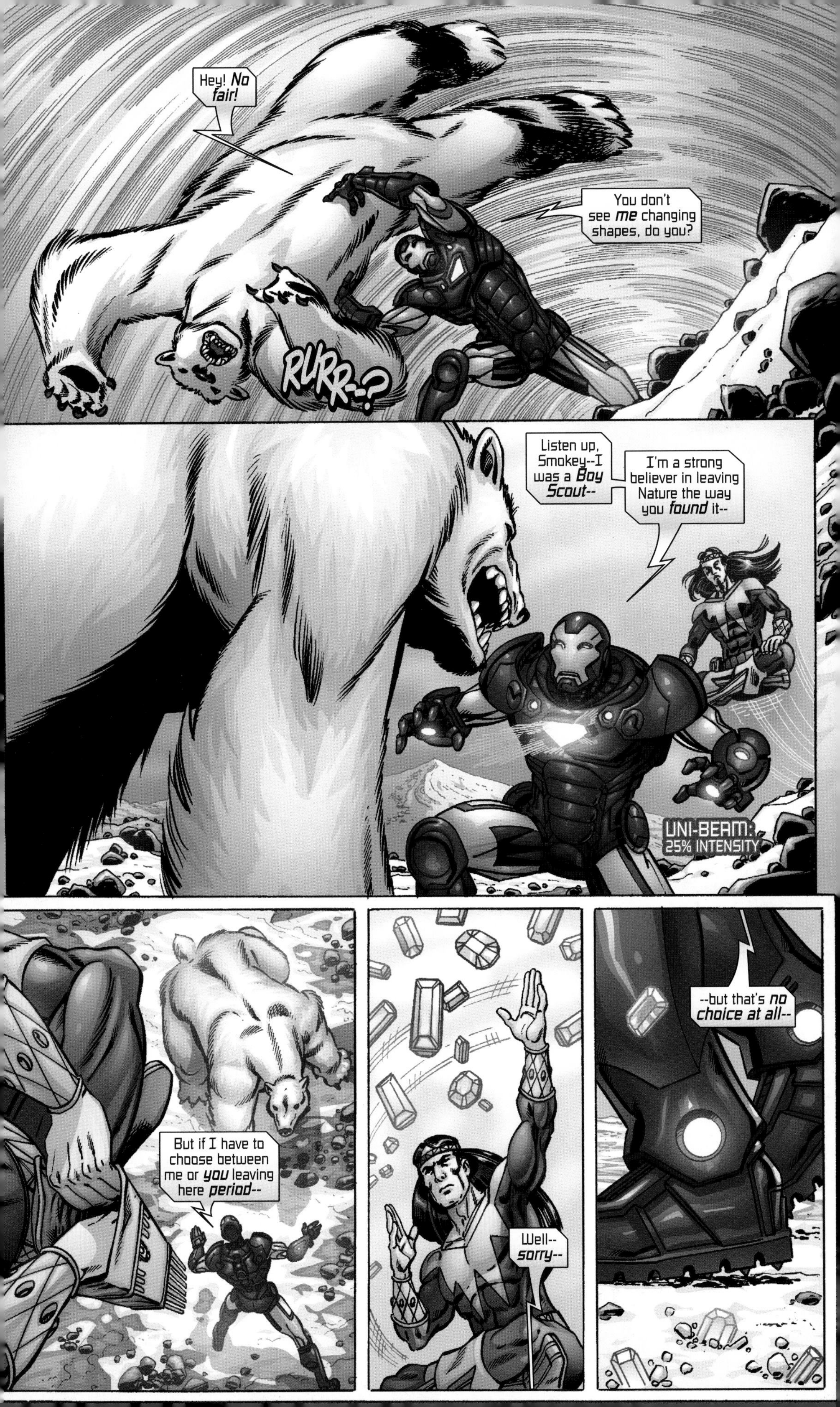

Hey! No fair!
You don't see me changing shapes, do you?
RURR--?
Listen up, Smokey--I was a Boy Scout--
I'm a strong believer in leaving Nature the way you found it--
UNI-BEAM: 25% INTENSITY
But if I have to choose between me or you leaving here period--
Well-- sorry--
--but that's no choice at all--

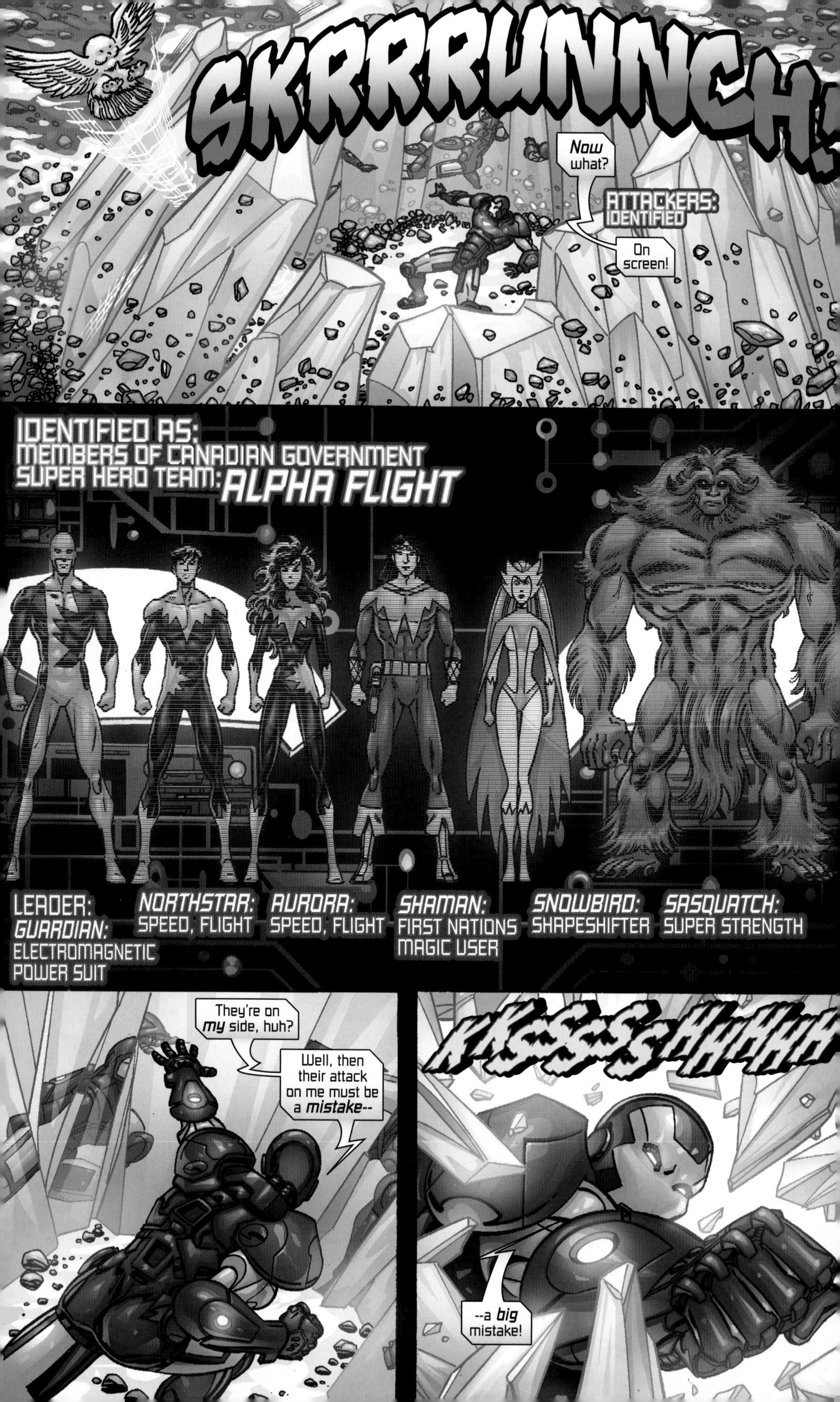
SKRRRUNNCH!
Now what?
ATTACKERS: IDENTIFIED
On screen!
IDENTIFIED AS: MEMBERS OF CANADIAN GOVERNMENT SUPER HERO TEAM: ALPHA FLIGHT
LEADER: GUARDIAN: ELECTROMAGNETIC POWER SUIT
NORTHSTAR: SPEED, FLIGHT
AURORA: SPEED, FLIGHT
SHAMAN: FIRST NATIONS MAGIC USER
SNOWBIRD: SHAPESHIFTER
SASQUATCH: SUPER STRENGTH
They're on *my* side, huh?
Well, then their attack on me must be a *mistake*--
--a *big* mistake!

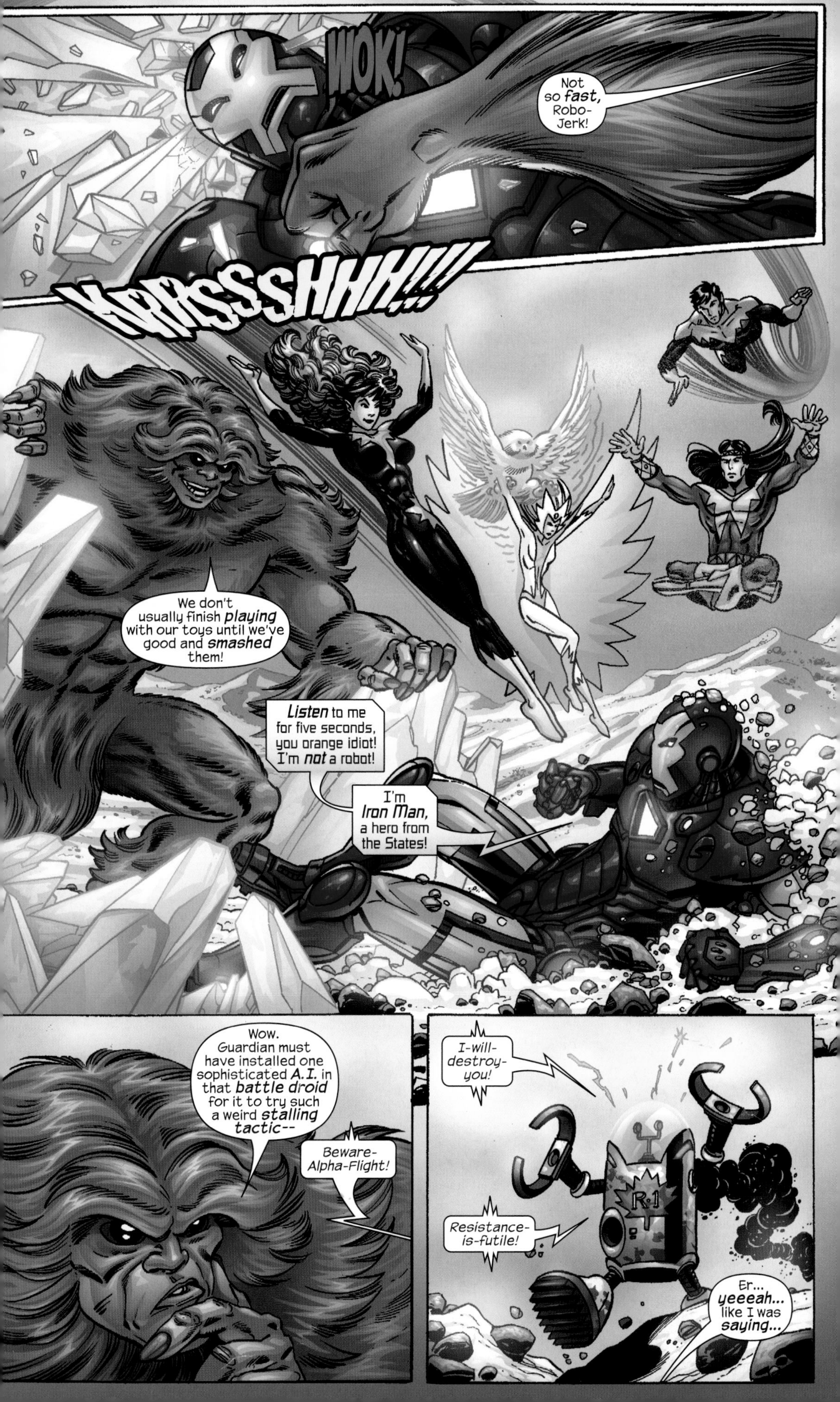

WOK!
Not so fast, Robo-Jerk!
KRRSSSHHH!!!
We don't usually finish playing with our toys until we've good and smashed them!
Listen to me for five seconds, you orange idiot! I'm not a robot!
I'm Iron Man, a hero from the States!
Wow. Guardian must have installed one sophisticated A.I. in that battle droid for it to try such a weird stalling tactic--
Beware-Alpha-Flight!
I-will-destroy-you!
Resistance-is-futile!
R-1
Er... yeeeah... like I was saying...

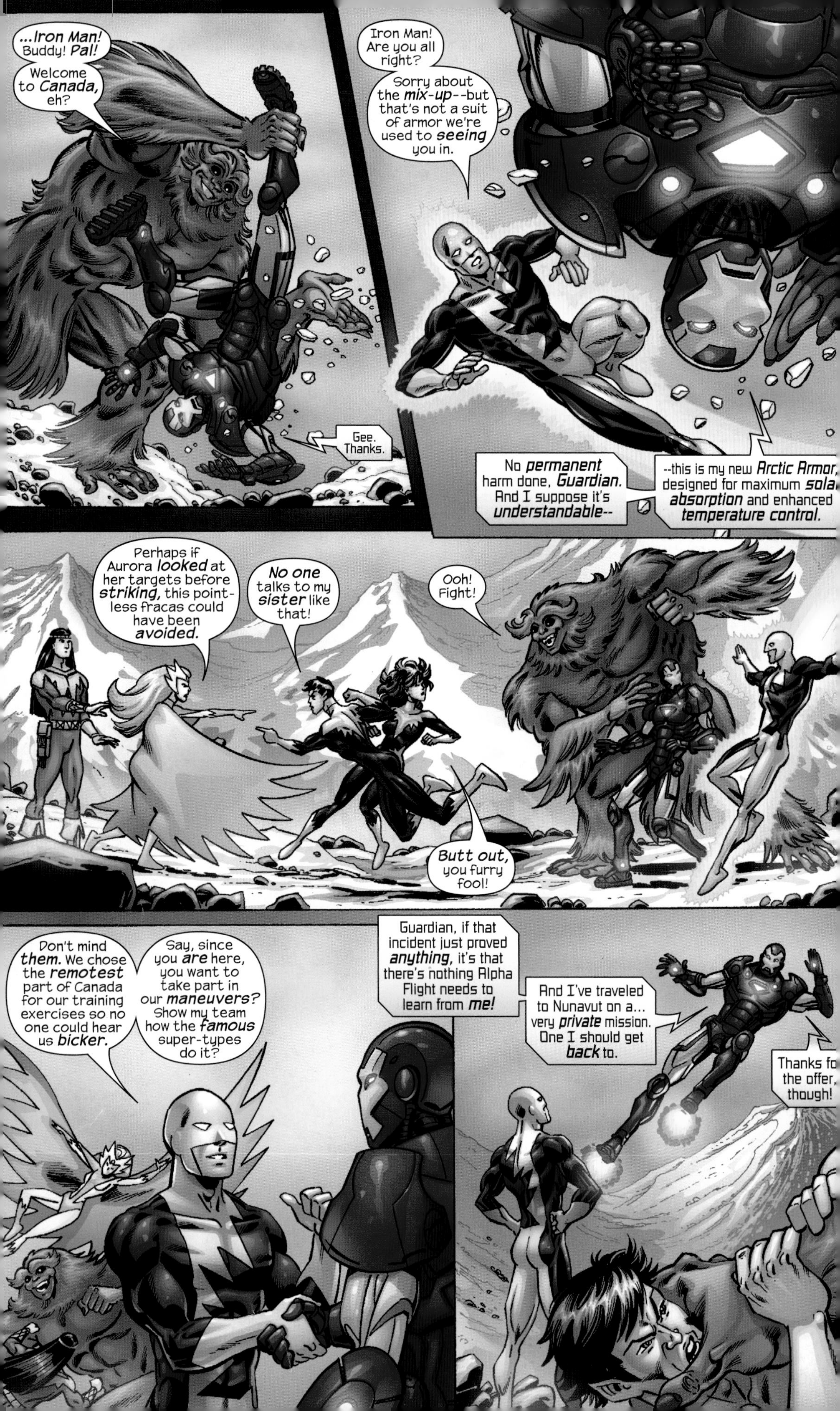
...Iron Man! Buddy! Pal!
Welcome to Canada, eh?
Gee. Thanks.
Iron Man! Are you all right?
Sorry about the mix-up--but that's not a suit of armor we're used to seeing you in.
No permanent harm done, Guardian. And I suppose it's understandable--
--this is my new Arctic Armor, designed for maximum sola absorption and enhanced temperature control.
Perhaps if Aurora looked at her targets before striking, this pointless fracas could have been avoided.
No one talks to my sister like that!
Ooh! Fight!
Butt out, you furry fool!
Don't mind them. We chose the remotest part of Canada for our training exercises so no one could hear us bicker.
Say, since you are here, you want to take part in our maneuvers? Show my team how the famous super-types do it?
Guardian, if that incident just proved anything, it's that there's nothing Alpha Flight needs to learn from me!
And I've traveled to Nunavut on a... very private mission. One I should get back to.
Thanks fo the offer, though!

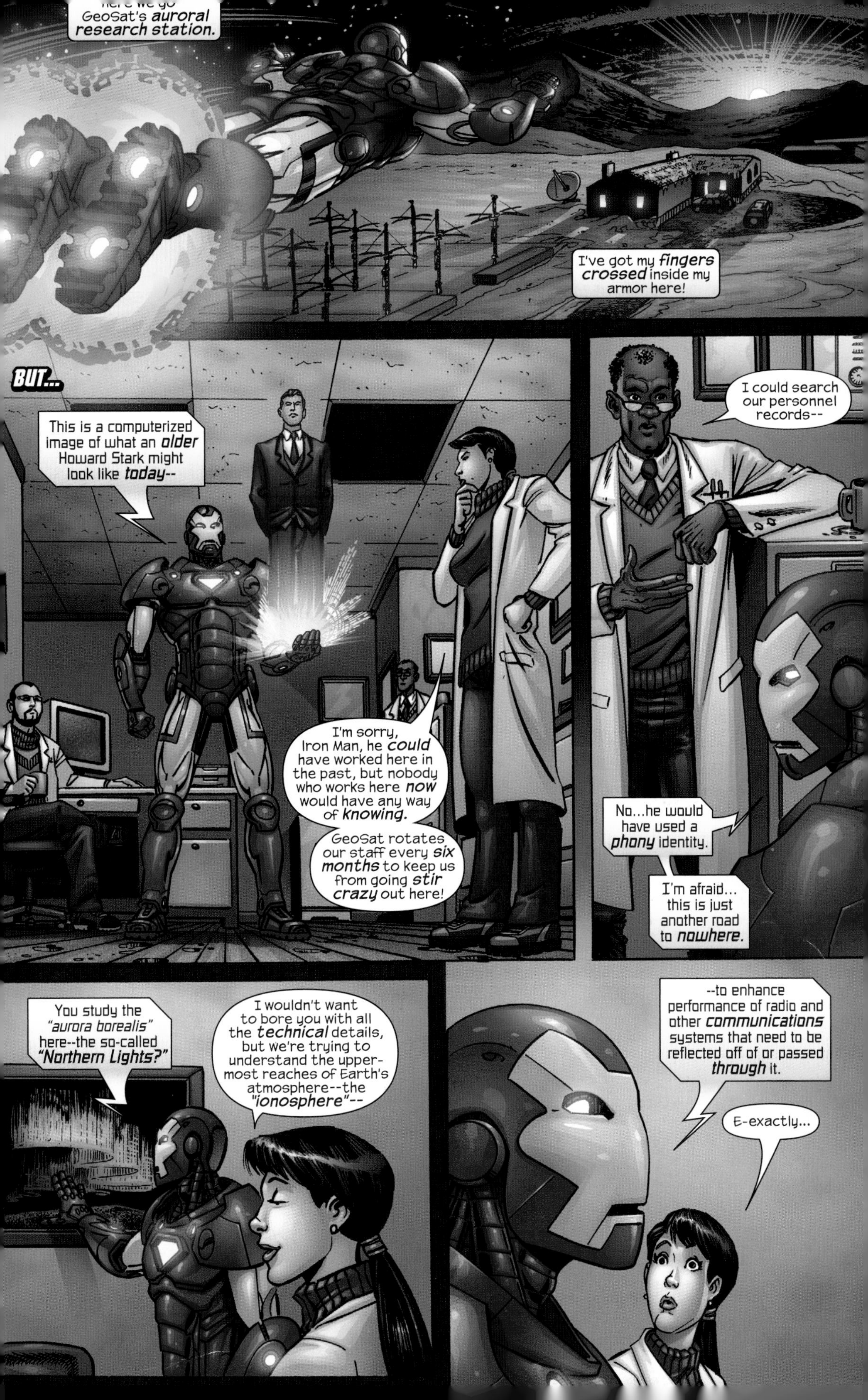
GeoSat's auroral research station.
I've got my fingers crossed inside my armor here!
BUT...
This is a computerized image of what an older Howard Stark might look like today--
I'm sorry, Iron Man, he could have worked here in the past, but nobody who works here now would have any way of knowing.
GeoSat rotates our staff every six months to keep us from going stir crazy out here!
I could search our personnel records--
No...he would have used a phony identity.
I'm afraid... this is just another road to nowhere.
You study the "aurora borealis" here--the so-called "Northern Lights?"
I wouldn't want to bore you with all the technical details, but we're trying to understand the upper-most reaches of Earth's atmosphere--the "ionosphere"--
--to enhance performance of radio and other communications systems that need to be reflected off of or passed through it.
E-exactly...

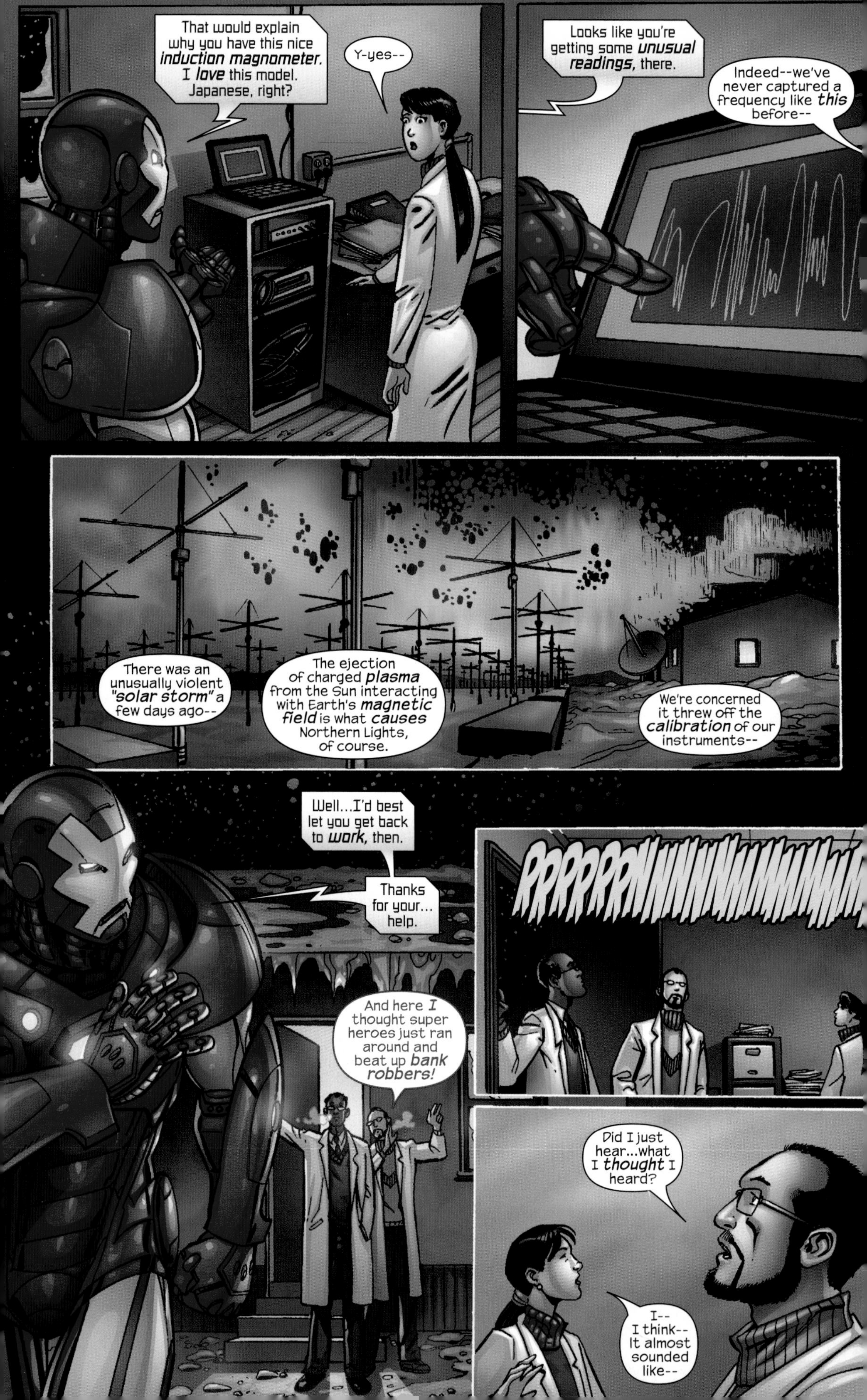
That would explain why you have this nice *induction magnometer*. I *love* this model. Japanese, right?
Y-yes--
Looks like you're getting some *unusual readings*, there.
Indeed--we've never captured a frequency like *this* before--
There was an unusually violent *"solar storm"* a few days ago--
The ejection of charged *plasma* from the Sun interacting with Earth's *magnetic field* is what *causes* Northern Lights, of course.
We're concerned it threw off the *calibration* of our instruments--
Well...I'd best let you get back to *work*, then.
Thanks for your... help.
And here *I* thought super heroes just ran around and beat up *bank robbers!*
RRRRRNNNNMMMMMM
Did I just hear...what I *thought* I heard?
I-- I think-- It almost sounded like--

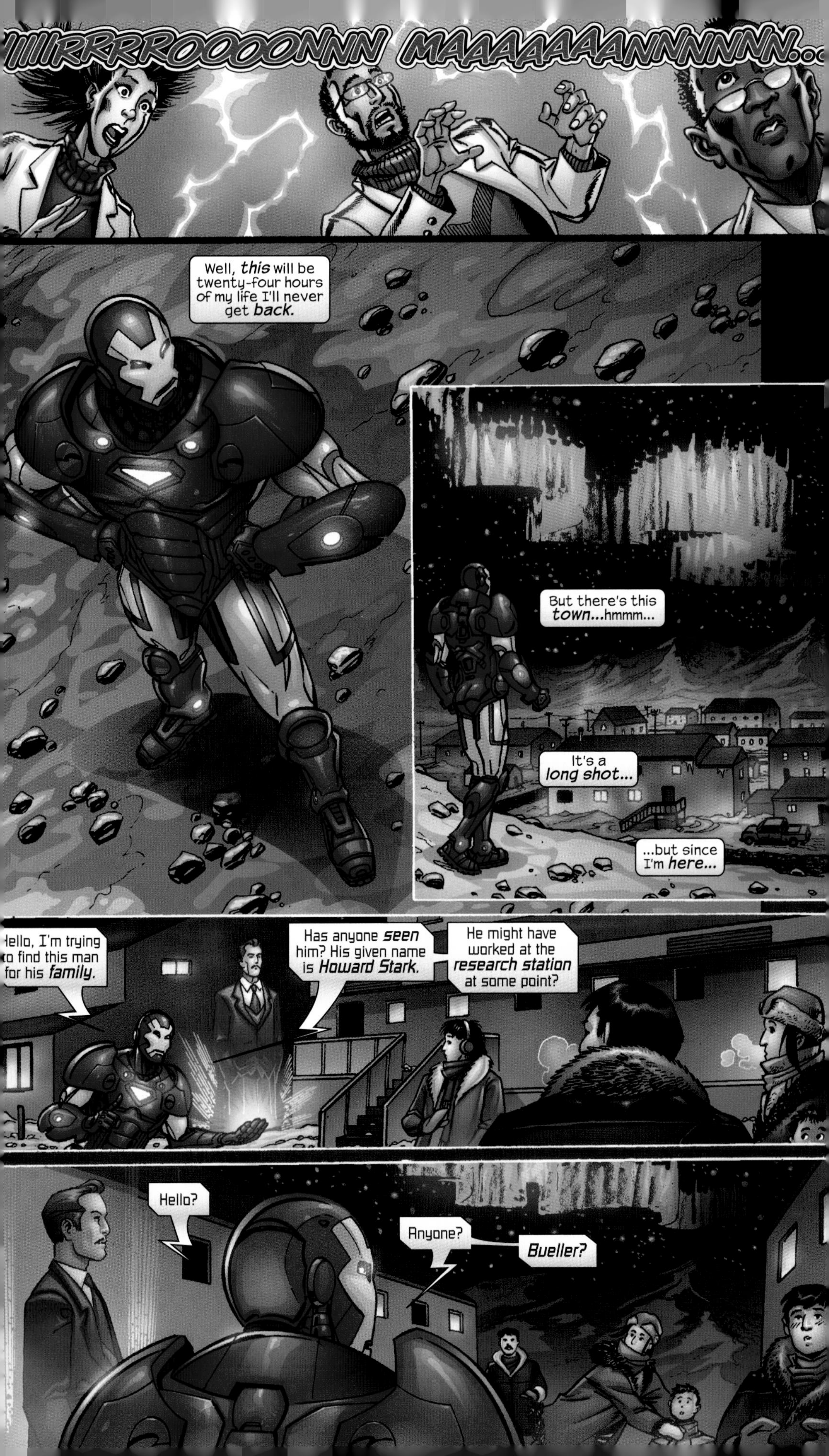
IIIIRRRROOOOONNN MAAAAAAANNNNNN...
Well, this will be twenty-four hours of my life I'll never get back.
But there's this town...hmmm...
It's a long shot...
...but since I'm here...
ello, I'm trying o find this man for his family.
Has anyone seen him? His given name is Howard Stark.
He might have worked at the research station at some point?
Hello?
Anyone?
Bueller?

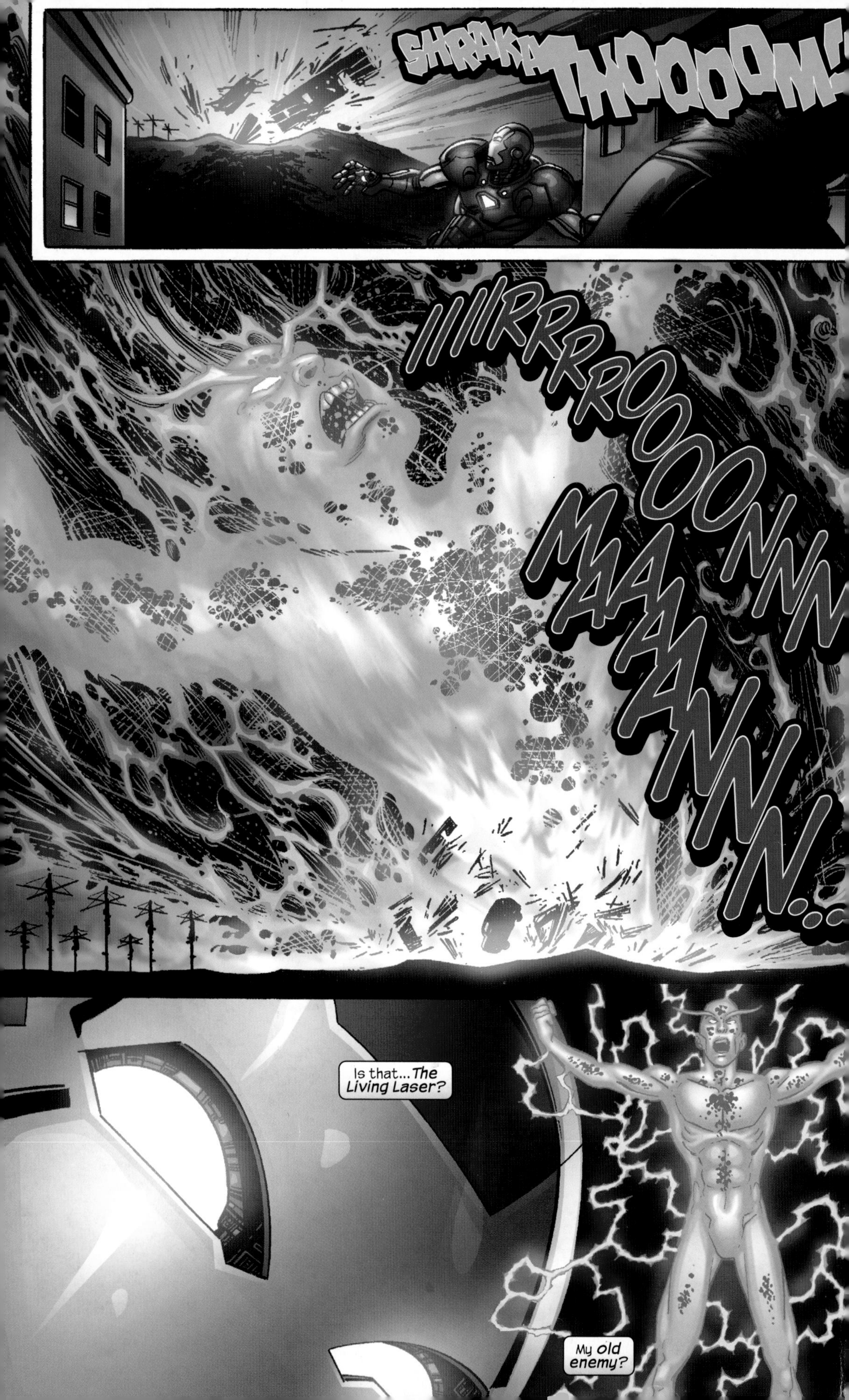
SHRAKATHOOOOM!
IIIIRRRROOOOONNN MAAAANNN...
Is that... The Living Laser?
My old enemy?

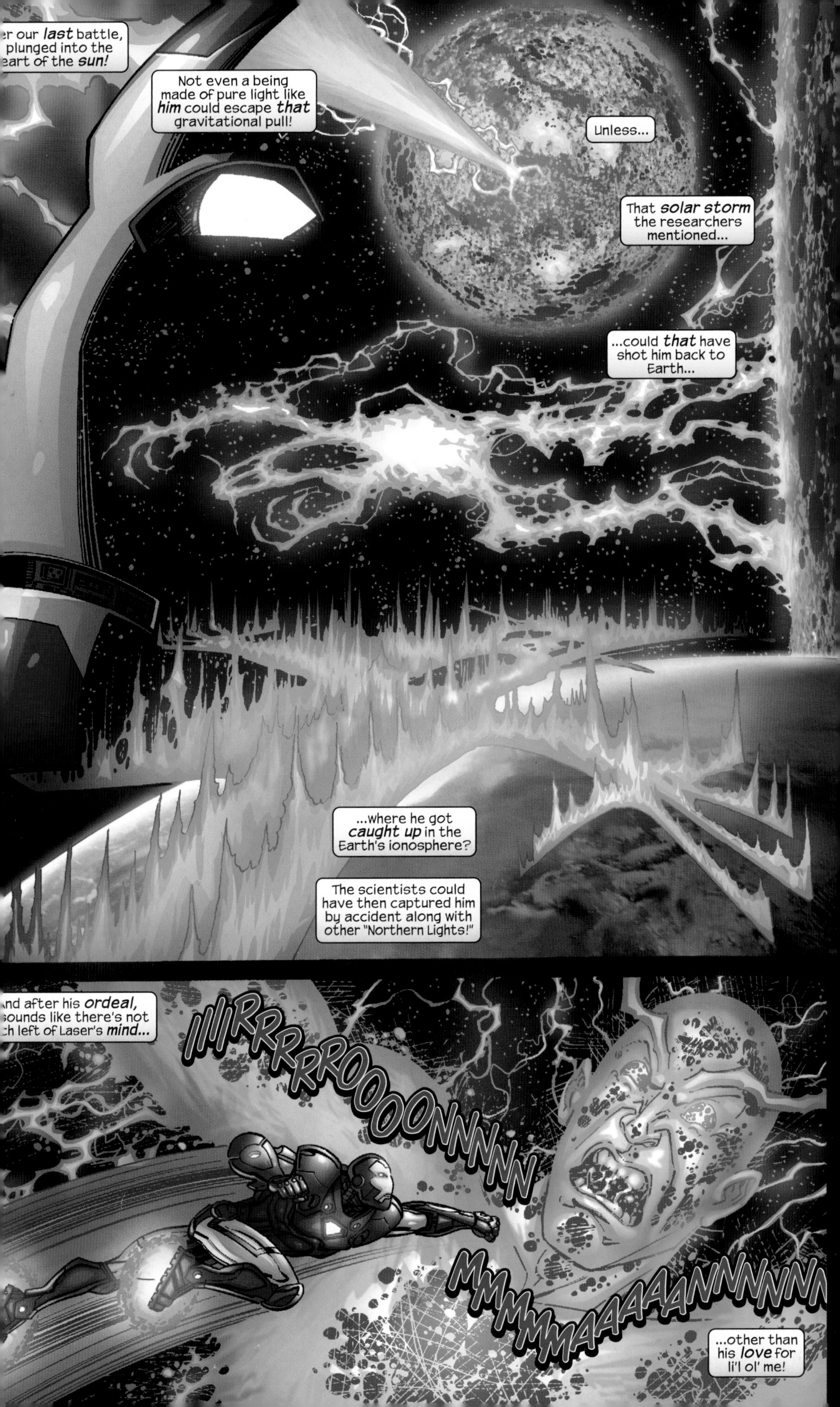

r our last battle, plunged into the eart of the sun!
Not even a being made of pure light like him could escape that gravitational pull!
Unless...
That solar storm the researchers mentioned...
...could that have shot him back to Earth...
...where he got caught up in the Earth's ionosphere?
The scientists could have then captured him by accident along with other "Northern Lights!"
nd after his ordeal, sounds like there's not ch left of Laser's mind...
IIIIRRRRROOOOONNNNNN
MMMMMAAAAAANNNNNNN
...other than his love for li'l ol' me!

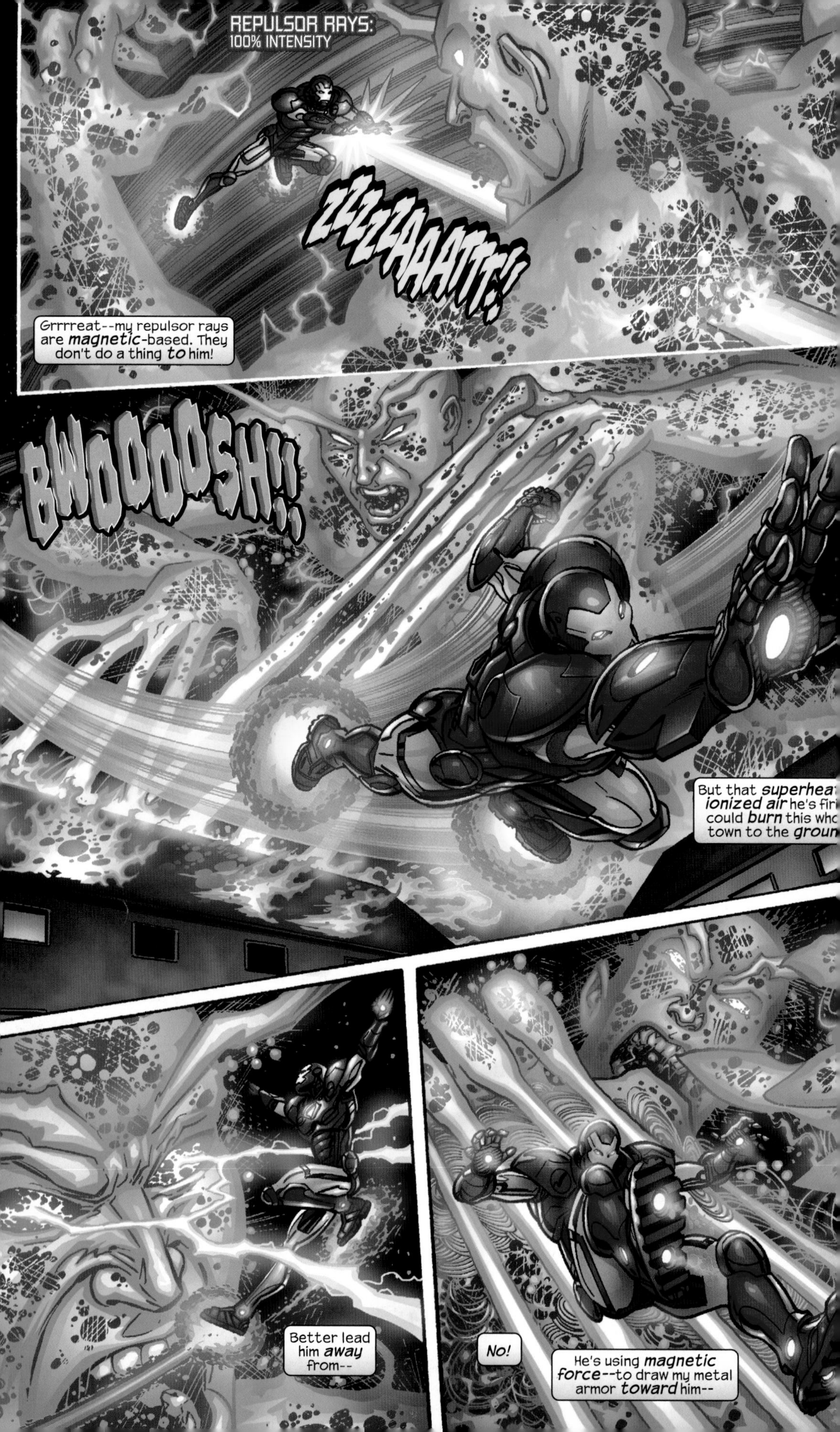
REPULSOR RAYS:
100% INTENSITY
ZZZZAAATTT!!
Grrrreat--my repulsor rays are magnetic-based. They don't do a thing to him!
BWOOOOSH!!
But that superheat ionized air he's fir could burn this who town to the groun
Better lead him away from--
No!
He's using magnetic force--to draw my metal armor toward him--

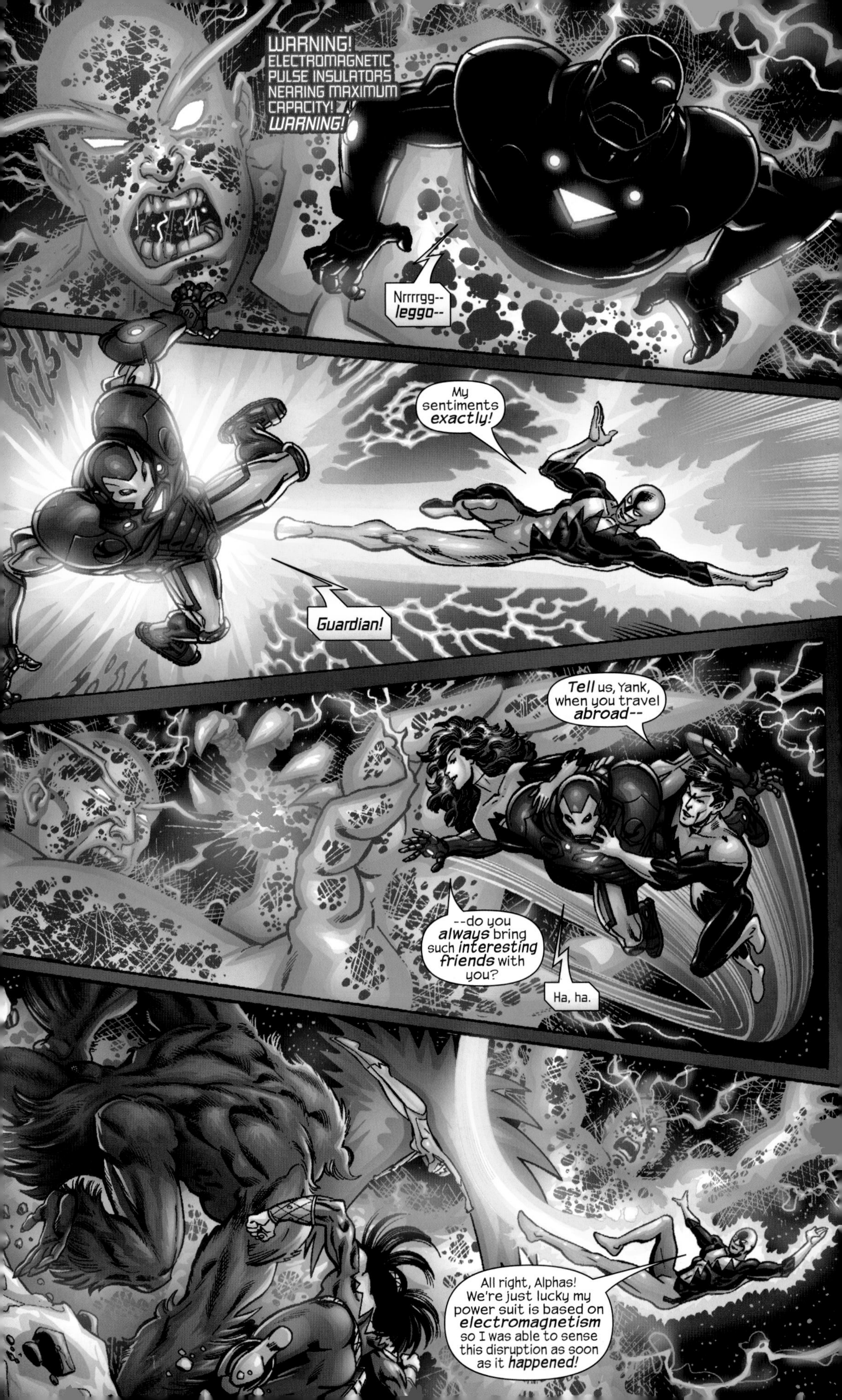

WARNING! ELECTROMAGNETIC PULSE INSULATORS NEARING MAXIMUM CAPACITY! WARNING!
Nrrrrgg-- leggo--
My sentiments exactly!
Guardian!
Tell us, Yank, when you travel abroad--
--do you always bring such interesting friends with you?
Ha, ha.
All right, Alphas! We're just lucky my power suit is based on electromagnetism so I was able to sense this disruption as soon as it happened!

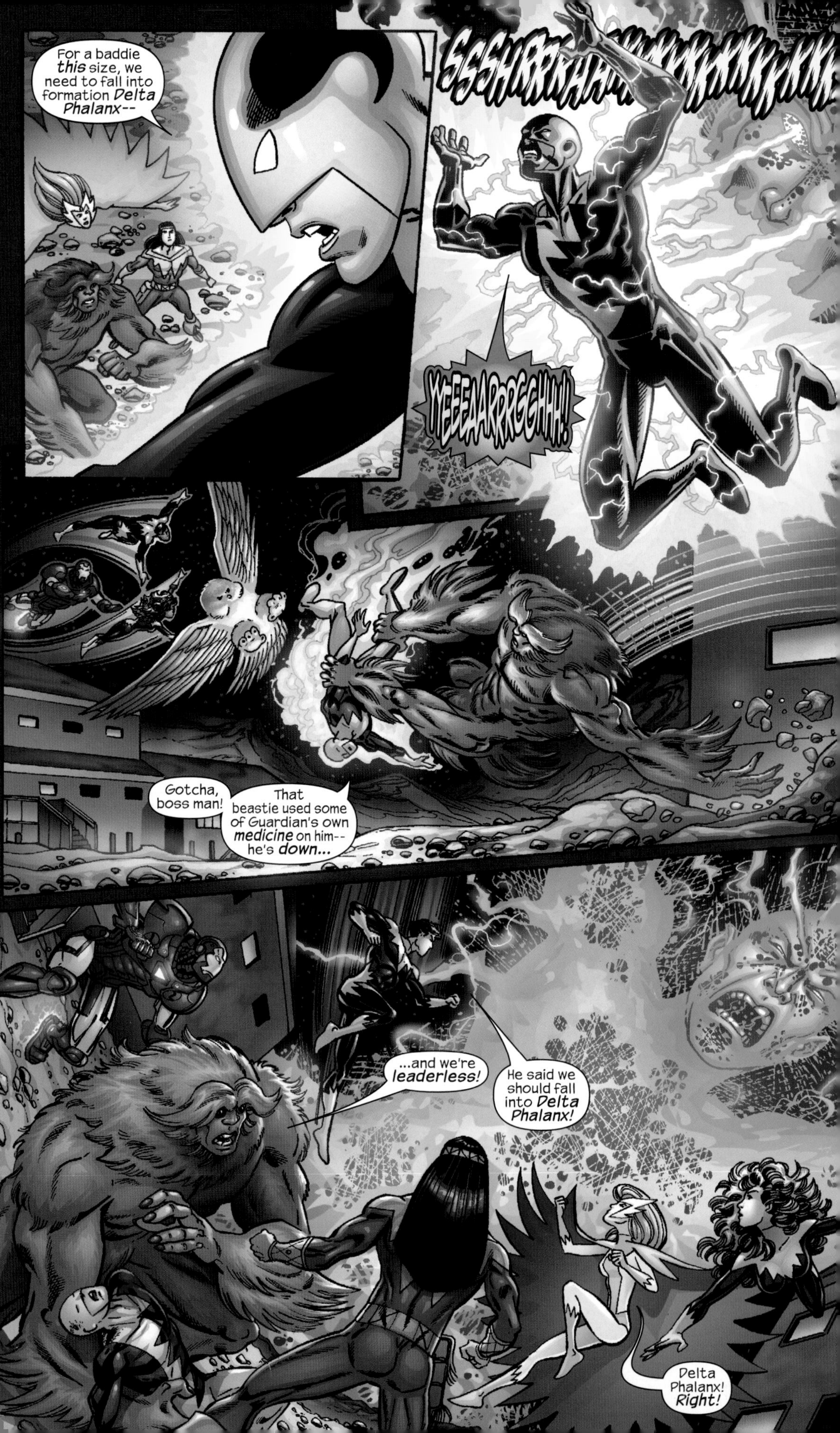

For a baddie this size, we need to fall into formation Delta Phalanx--
YYEEEAARRRGGHHH!
Gotcha, boss man!
That beastie used some of Guardian's own medicine on him-- he's down...
...and we're leaderless!
He said we should fall into Delta Phalanx!
Delta Phalanx! Right!

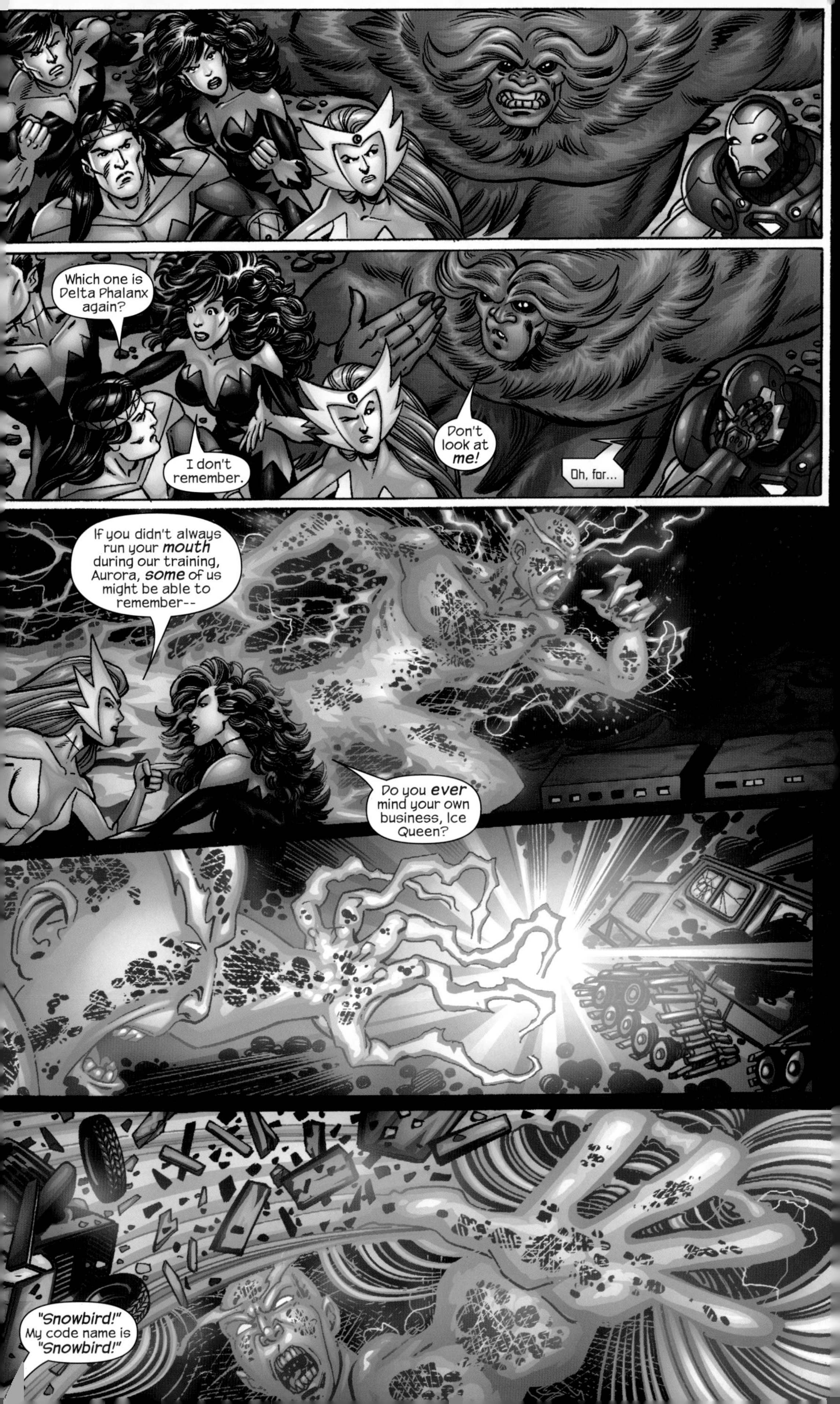
Which one is Delta Phalanx again?
I don't remember.
Don't look at me!
Oh, for...
If you didn't always run your mouth during our training, Aurora, some of us might be able to remember--
Do you ever mind your own business, Ice Queen?
"Snowbird!" My code name is "Snowbird!"

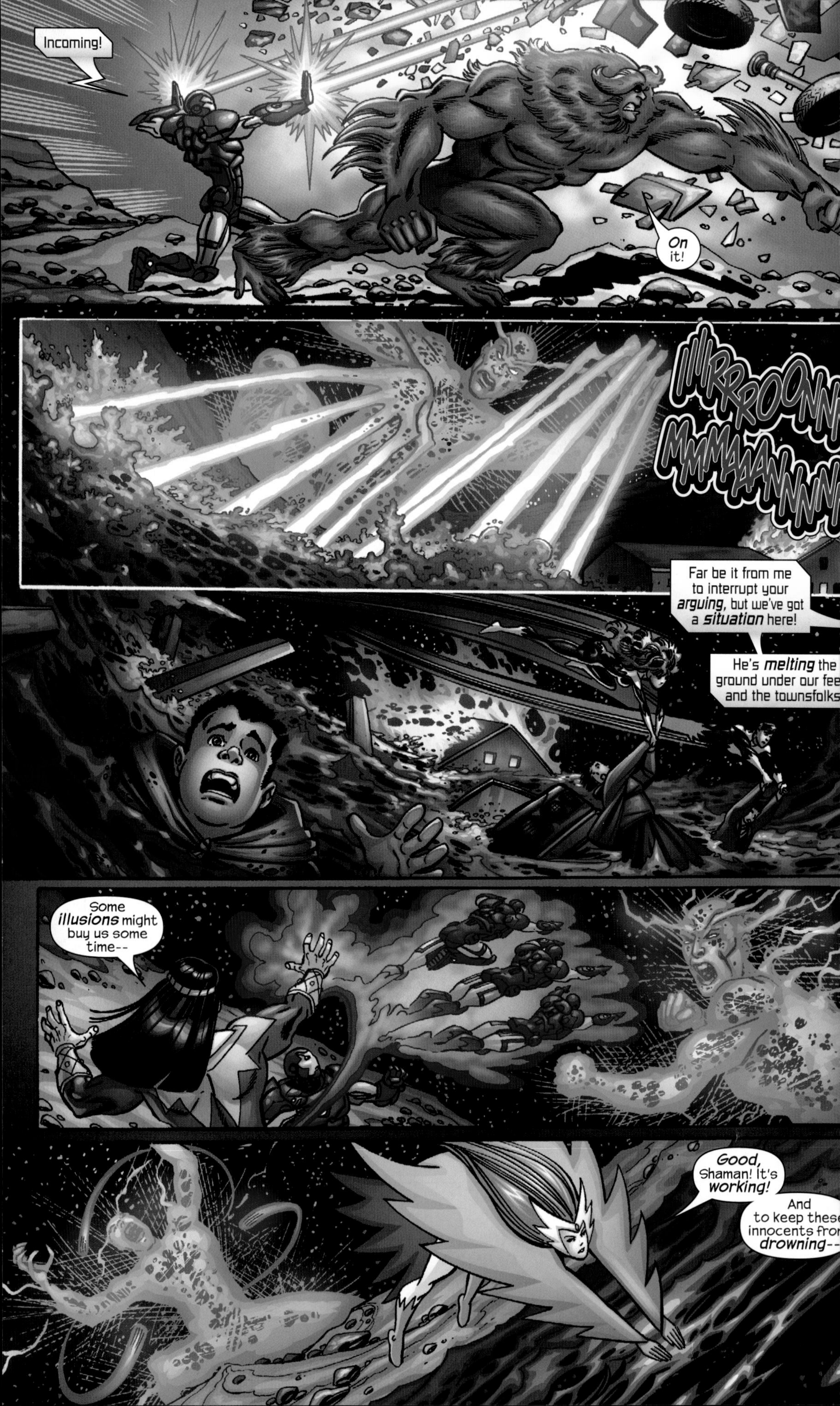
Incoming!
On it!
IIIIRRROONNN MMMAAANNNN
Far be it from me to interrupt your *arguing*, but we've got a *situation* here!
He's *melting* the ground under our fee and the townsfolks
Some *illusions* might buy us some time--
Good, Shaman! It's *working!*
And to keep these innocents fron *drowning*--

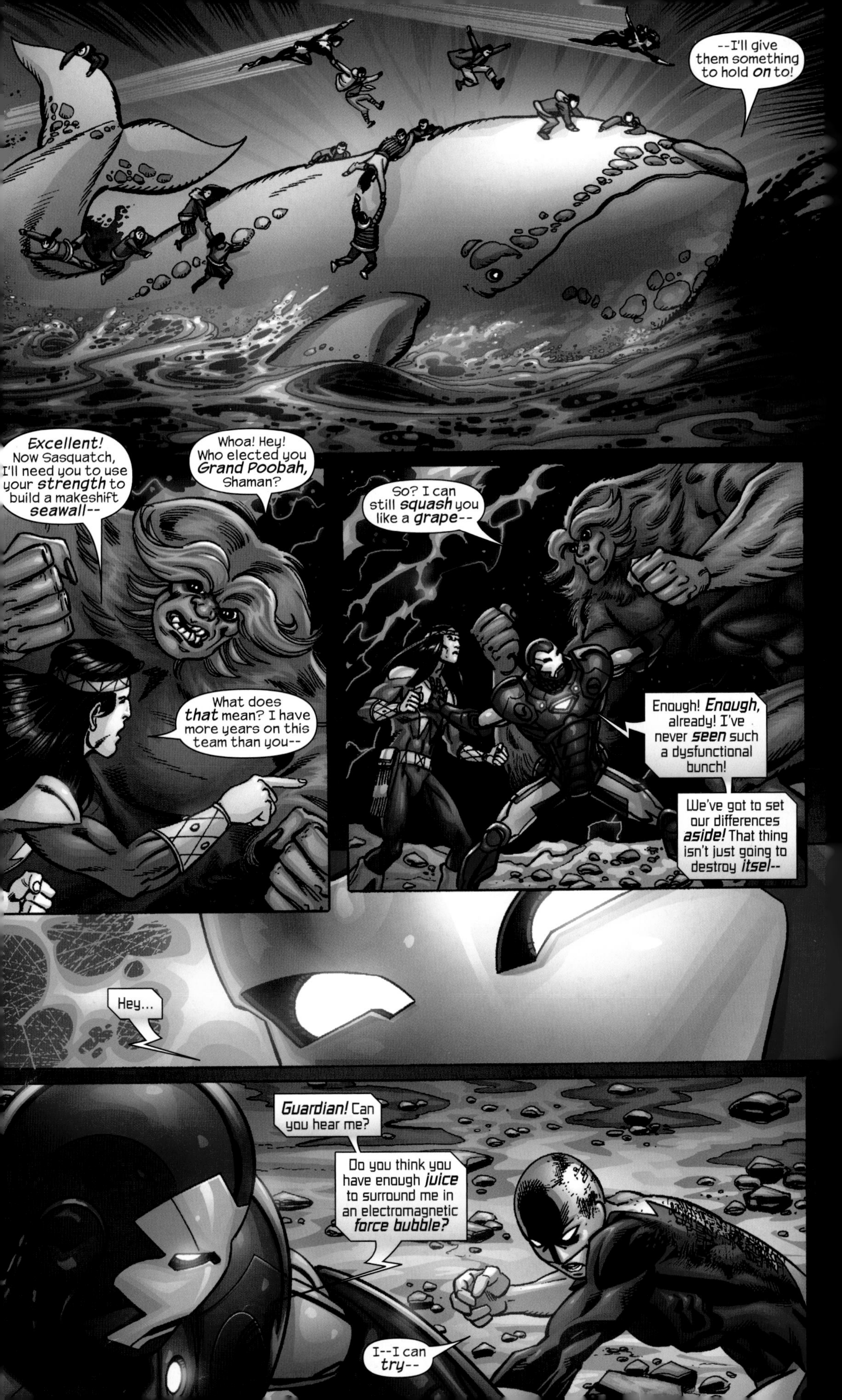

--I'll give them something to hold *on* to!
Excellent! Now Sasquatch, I'll need you to use your *strength* to build a makeshift *seawall*--
Whoa! Hey! Who elected you *Grand Poobah,* Shaman?
What does *that* mean? I have more years on this team than you--
So? I can still *squash* you like a *grape*--
Enough! *Enough,* already! I've never *seen* such a dysfunctional bunch!
We've got to set our differences *aside!* That thing isn't just going to destroy *itsel*--
Hey...
Guardian! Can you hear me?
Do you think you have enough *juice* to surround me in an electromagnetic *force bubble?*
I--I can *try*--

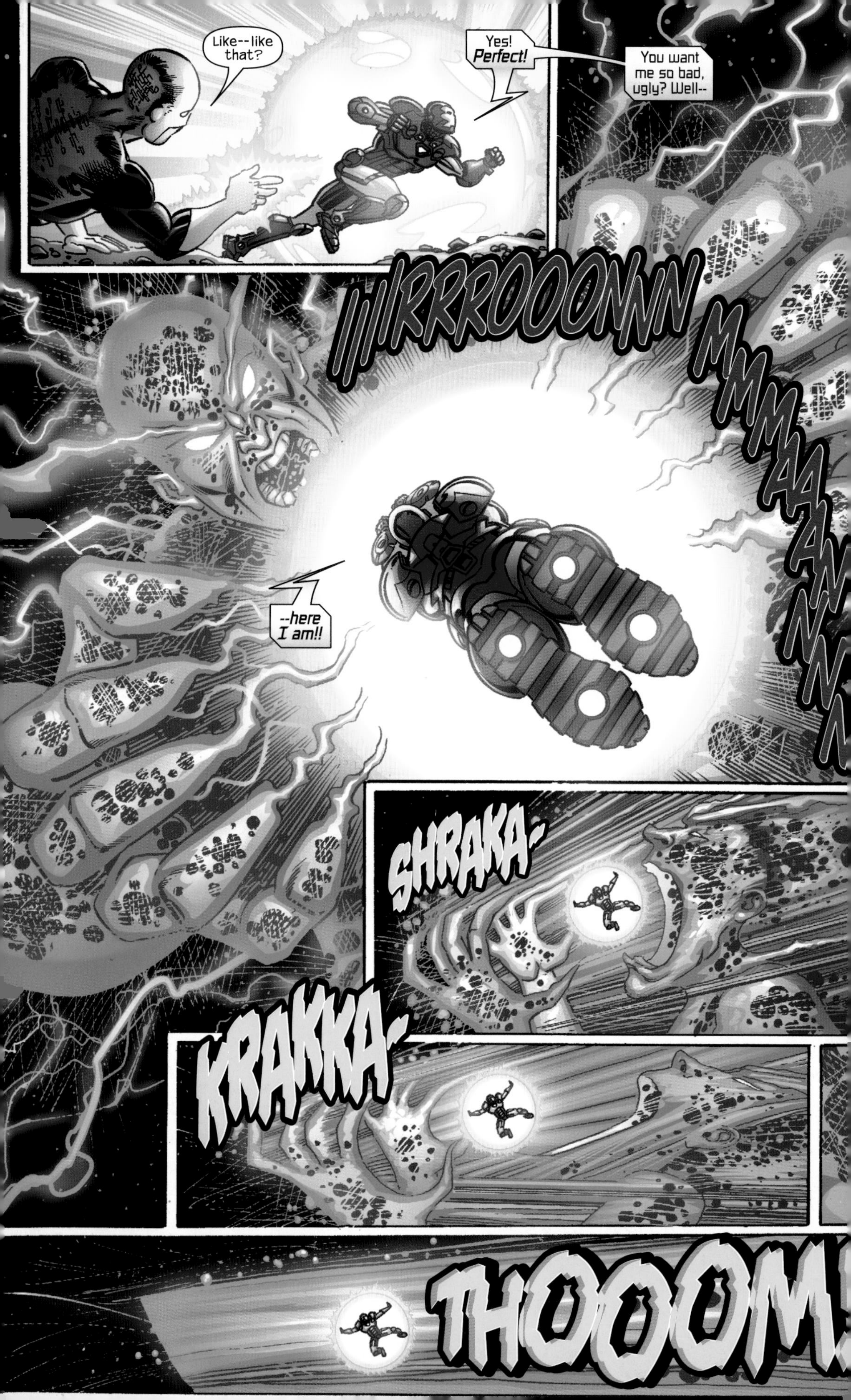

Like--like that?
Yes! *Perfect!*
You want me so bad, ugly? Well--
IIIRRROOONNN MMMAAANNNN
--here I am!!
SHRAKA-
KRAKKA-
THOOOM!

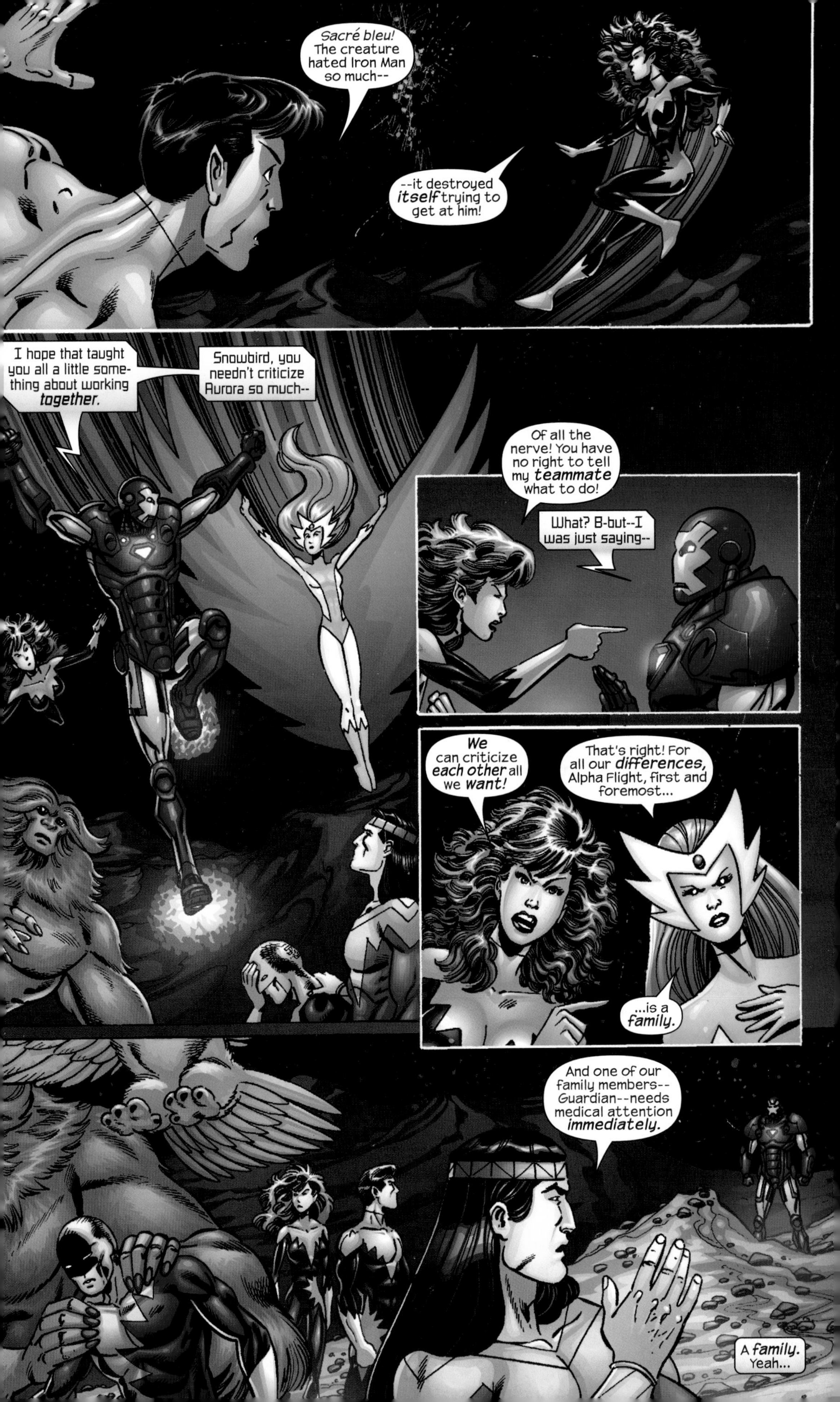

Sacré bleu! The creature hated Iron Man so much--
--it destroyed *itself* trying to get at him!
I hope that taught you all a little something about working *together.*
Snowbird, you needn't criticize Aurora so much--
Of all the nerve! You have no right to tell my *teammate* what to do!
What? B-but--I was just saying--
We can criticize *each other* all we *want!*
That's right! For all our *differences,* Alpha Flight, first and foremost...
...is a *family.*
And one of our family members--Guardian--needs medical attention *immediately.*
A *family.* Yeah...

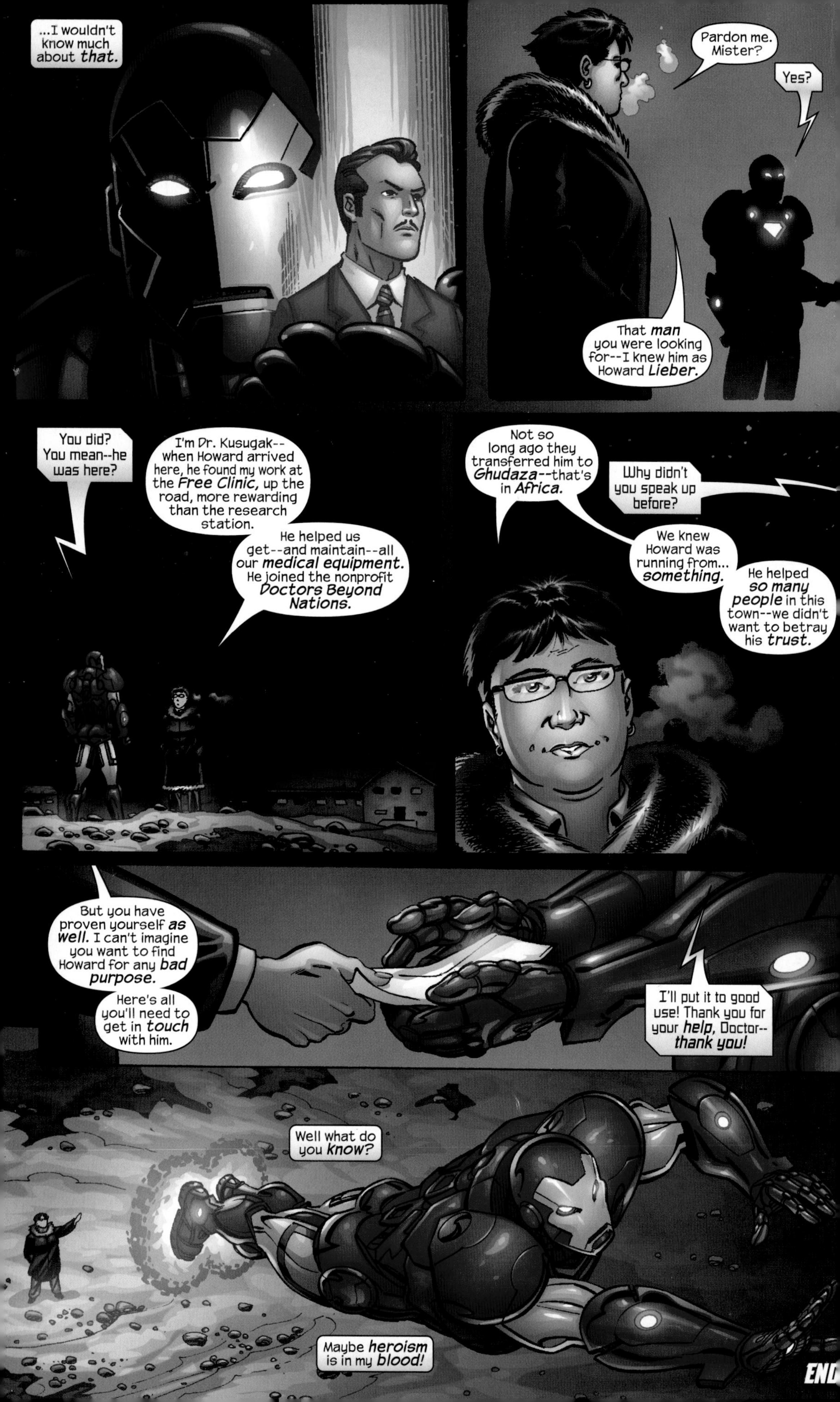
...I wouldn't know much about *that.*
Pardon me. Mister?
Yes?
That *man* you were looking for--I knew him as Howard *Lieber.*
You did? You mean--he was here?
I'm Dr. Kusugak--when Howard arrived here, he found my work at the *Free Clinic,* up the road, more rewarding than the research station.
He helped us get--and maintain--all our *medical equipment.* He joined the nonprofit *Doctors Beyond Nations.*
Not so long ago they transferred him to *Ghudaza*--that's in *Africa.*
Why didn't you speak up before?
We knew Howard was running from... *something.*
He helped *so many people* in this town--we didn't want to betray his *trust.*
But you have proven yourself *as well.* I can't imagine you want to find Howard for any *bad purpose.*
Here's all you'll need to get in *touch* with him.
I'll put it to good use! Thank you for your *help,* Doctor--*thank you!*
Well what do you *know?*
Maybe *heroism* is in my *blood!*
END